Hide-and-Seek

My Little Pony: Hide-and-Seek

Text and illustrations copyright © 2005 by Hasbro, Inc., HASBRO and its logo and MY LITTLE PONY and all related characters are trademarks of Hasbro and are used with permission.

This 2010 edition was created exclusively for Sandy Creek by arrangement with HarperCollins Publishers.

HarperCollins Publishers® and I Can Read Books® are registered trademarks.

Sandy Creek
122 Fifth Avenue
New York, NY 10011

ISBN 978-1-4351-2650-3
Manufactured in China.
Manufactured 05/2010
Lot 10 11 12 13 SCP 10 9 8 7 6 5 4 3 2

birdbath

mushroom

ears

nose

eyes

quilt

feet

rosebush

flower

shed

frog

sun

grasshopper

tail

kite

tea

ladybug

tree

"What a fun day

to play outside!"

said Petal Blossom.

The ☀ was high

in the sky.

And all the 🌳

and the 🌸

were in full bloom.

"What should we do today?"

asked Sparkleworks.

"Let's fly a ☐ !" said

Meadowbrook.

"Let's pick ❀❀ !"

said Star Swirl.

"I know," said Petal Blossom.

"Let's play hide-and-seek!"

"I'll be *it*," said

Meadowbrook.

She started to count,

"1 . . . 2 . . . 3 . . ."

When she got to ten,

she opened her

and said, "Ready or not,

here I come!"

Meadowbrook saw

Petal Blossom first.

Her  was sticking

out from behind a  .

Meadowbrook tagged her

friend's  playfully.

"I found you, Petal

Blossom!"

"I am always the first to be found!" Petal Blossom said, smiling.

Next, Meadowbrook saw Sweetberry's poking out of a .

"Gotcha, Sweetberry!"

Next, Meadowbrook looked

behind the  .

Then she looked behind the  .

Where are my friends

hiding? she wondered.

Soon she saw Star Swirl's

 beneath a  .

"You are tagged, Star Swirl,"

said Sweetberry.

But where was Sparkleworks?

"We will help you find her!"

said Star Swirl.

Sweetberry found a 🦗.

Star Swirl found a little 🐸.

Petal Blossom found a 🐞.

But none of the ponies could

find Sparkleworks.

Can you?

"Sparkleworks is the best hider!" Meadowbrook whispered to the other three ponies. "If *we* can't find her, maybe we can make *her* find us. Let's have a 🍵 party!"

Petal Blossom got

the ![blanket].

Star Swirl gathered

pretty ![flowers] in a bunch.

Sweetberry poured

make-believe ![teacup].

Soon Sparkleworks heard

laughter in her .

She smelled the scent of

 in her .

Then Sparkleworks'

peeked out.

She saw her friends

on the

having a fun  party.

Sparkleworks came out of

her hiding place.

"Hiding is fun," she said.

"But finding your friends

is even better!"